Bob
is a
Unicorn

By Michelle Nelson-Schmidt

Kane Miller
A DIVISION OF EDC PUBLISHING

*Dedicated to all the hopers,
the dreamers and the ones of us that
don't quite fit so neatly
into a category or definition.*

Kane Miller, A Division of EDC Publishing

Text and illustrations copyright © Michelle Nelson-Schmidt 2013

For information contact:
Kane Miller, A Division of EDC Publishing
PO Box 470663
Tulsa, OK 74147-0663
www.kanemiller.com
www.edcpub.com
usbornebooksandmore.com

Library of Congress Control Number: 2012944941

Manufactured by Regent Publishing Services, Hong Kong
Printed February 2015 in ShenZhen, Guangdong, China

Hardcover ISBN: 978-1-61067-155-2
Paperback ISBN: 978-1-61067-189-7

Bob is not a unicorn.
Everyone can see that.
Everyone but Bob.

Whoa, Bob. What are you
supposed to be?

*I'm a unicorn, Marvin.
Can't you tell?*

No.

Well, I am.

Hey, Bob.

Hey, Stella.

What are you supposed to be?

You can't tell?

No.

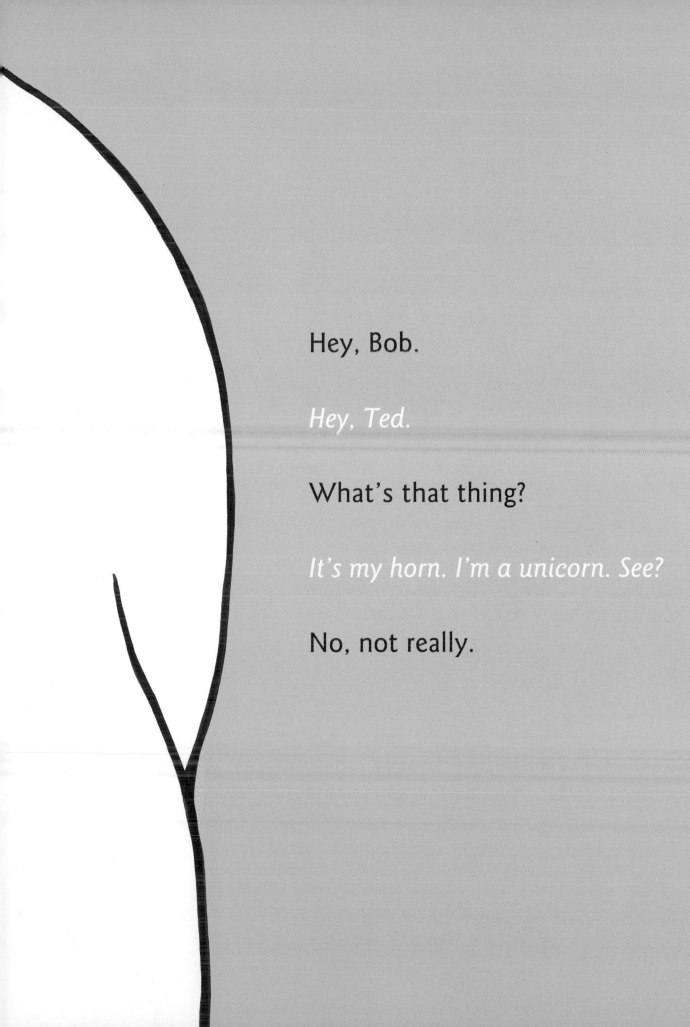

Hey, Bob.

Hey, Ted.

What's that thing?

It's my horn. I'm a unicorn. See?

No, not really.

Margo, you can tell what I am, right?

Besides silly?

George, I don't suppose you—

Bob, don't you have more important things to do?

I'm being a unicorn today.

It looks like you're wasting time to me.

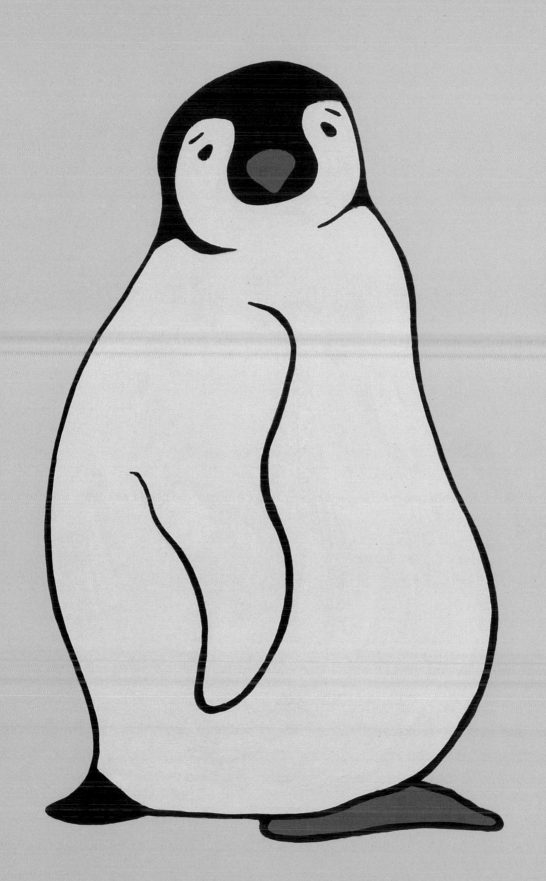

Henry, look at me. Guess what I am.

Bob, I've been up since the crack of dawn.

Sorry, Henry.

Hi, Francis. Can you guess what I am?

I'm too old to play games, Bob.
Why don't you just tell me what you are.
I have things to do.

Never mind.

Hi, Larry. What are you doing?

Working, Bob. I'm working.
What is that? What are you up to?

I'm playing. It's—

I'm busy, Bob.

Bye, Larry.

Oh well.

Oh!

Look at you.
You are the best unicorn
I've ever seen.
What a beautiful horn.
And just look at your
mane. And the sparkles.

Let's play, Bob.

Yes, please.

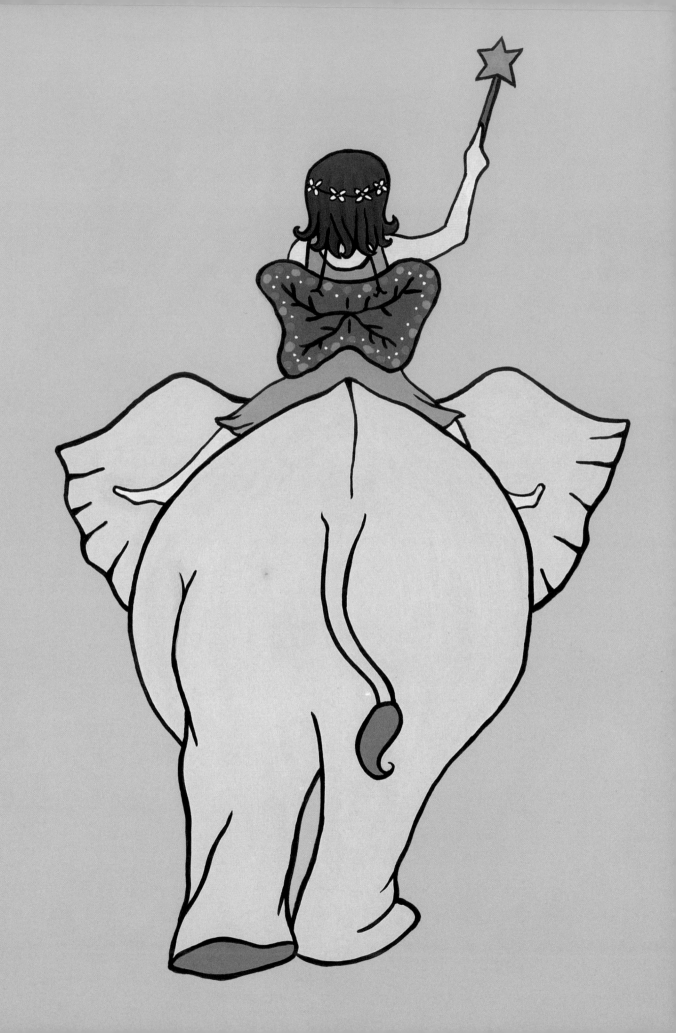

Make this a personal audio book!

To get started:
1. Download the free StorySticker app, or visit www.storysticker.com
2. Set up an account
3. Scan or enter the code below
4. Record yourself reading the story one page at a time and save when finished

Great for any child to read along with parents, grandparents or whomever they choose!

KGSBFGBXWG

StorySticker™
all you read is love